the FARMER

Story & Illustrations By
MARK LUDY

Green Pastures Publishing, Inc.
Longmont, Colorado

Illustrations and Text copyright © 1998
Green Pastures Publishing, Inc.
All Rights Reserved

ISBN 0 – 9664276 – 0 – 2

Library of Congress Catalog Card Number:
98 – 73805

Printed in China

Published by:

Green Pastures Publishing, Inc.
P.O. Box 1808
Longmont, CO 80502
(303) 684-9118
(888) 871-8694
Email: paul@greenpastures.com
Website: http://www.greenpastures.com

Dedicated to

Jeremy, it was you who inspired this book

My future wifey poo out there
whoever and wherever you are... I love ya

and to my family (though I might be biased
you all are the greatest

There are several people I would wish to thank

Paul and Sue Farabaugh, You have no idea how much
appreciate you two. Thank you for hangin' in there with
me, encouraging me and believing in me. This book would
not have been completed if it weren't for you

Pat Brunner, your help was such a wonderful gift to u

To all my friends out there... (you know who you are!
Thank you! Thank you! Thank you
...Do you know how I feel about you?

Thank you Mawie and Da-ee! Your words have helped shap
me, your examples have inspired me and your love ha
touched me. Thank you for being just the way your are
I am honored to be called your son

And most importantly, my Lord, I thank you. Always yo
have been the lifter of my chin and my chief delight in lif
is knowing you

the

FARMER

Can you smell that?

That's fresh country goodness, wholesome garden aromas, and an unmistakable pig smell. The old man with the fluffy white beard and big blue overalls is the farmer. This farm has been his home for many years. He makes his living by raising fresh vegetables and fruit and selling them at the market.

Every morning it's the same.
Millibell, the cow, comes to the
gate to greet her master. She
nuzzles his arm and snuggles up
close to hear his gentle voice
whispering his love to her. The
farmer gives her an affectionate
scratching behind her ears.

Millibell faithfully gives her friend
creamy, delicious milk.

Churchill, the clever quacker, is a yellow bundle of fun and feather-fluff. The farmer holds the little duck dear to his heart.

A pail of nourishing slop is just what Patsy, the farmer's curly-tailed piggy, loves for dinner. Patsy also loves to be tickled in just the right place.

Have you noticed Squeakers? He's the farmer's constant companion.

Tending the growing plants and pulling out weeds is the farmer's very important job. If all goes well, there will be plenty of fruit and vegetables for him to take to market. If all goes well...

At the end of a good day's work, it's time to get warm and cozy by the fire. The farmer savors a bowl of hot stew while his purring cat Clyde and little Squeakers keep him company.

As he does every night, he kneels into two worn grooves on the floor and lifts his heart in prayer.

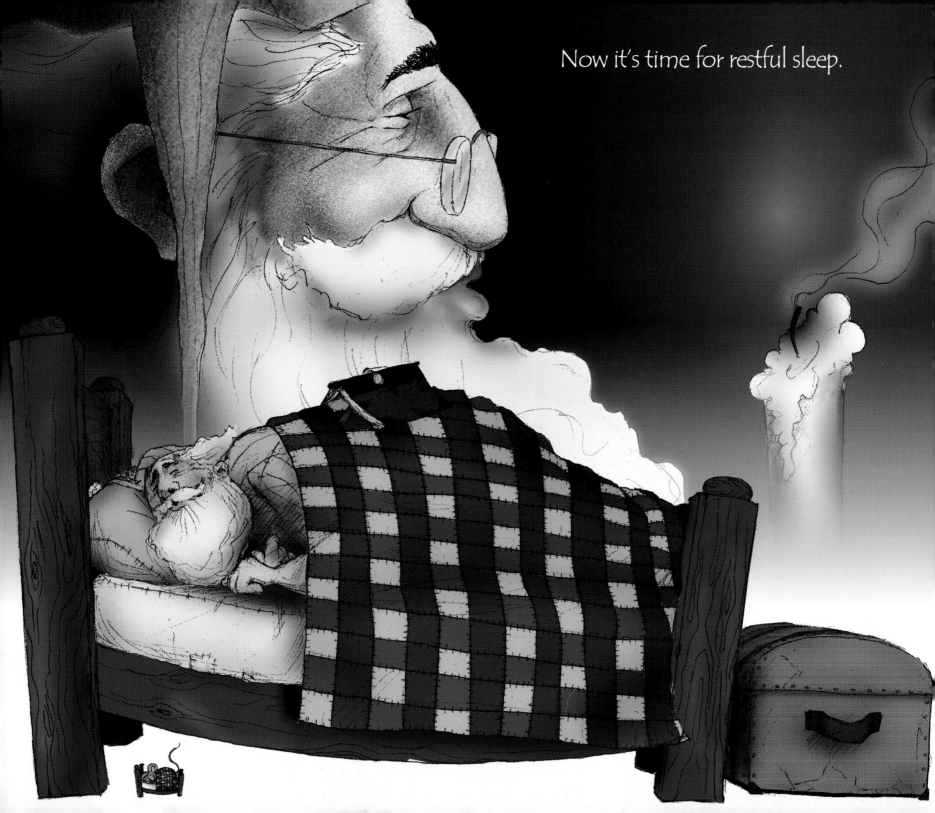

Now it's time for restful sleep.

What is that sound?
In an instant, the farmer is wide awake.

Rushing to the door, he looks out and beholds a frightening sight.

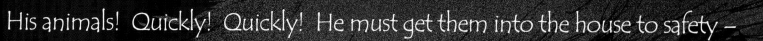
His animals! Quickly! Quickly! He must get them into the house to safety –

before the twisting funnel of madness arrives!

A soft beam of early morning sunlight breaks through the rafters and bathes the farmer with its warmth, slowly awakening him.

Stumbling outside into the morning air, he stops, stunned. Everything…everything is gone!

The farmer falls to his knees upon the muddy ground.

Tears stream down his face.

He had thought the shelves would be full for winter, but now they are bare. He will need money for food and supplies to repair his farm and seeds for next year's crop. He must sell his Millibell.

Poor Millibell does not understand. The farmer's neighbors, the Frumps, are reluctant to part with their money but are eager to own such a fine cow. With this money, the farmer can fix the storm's damage and buy a little food for the winter.

His heart still aching for Millibell, the farmer goes home to rebuild.

It is a harsh winter.

Spring arrives with freshness and new hope. Perhaps this year will bring an abundant harvest, enough for him to have plenty to buy back his cow.

A farmer needs sunshine…and rain. How wonderful this year will be!

He prepares the ground for the planting of seeds. Each day brings the farmer new challenges, hard work…and sweat as he cares for his garden.

For a good day's work and rest to come, the farmer offers thanks.

What's that smell? What could be burning?

The Frump boys have set the garden ablaze.

Hurry! Hurry! Try to save…

Morning light slips over the horizon. The fire is out but the crops are gone…again.

All is lost.

Hopes for a comfortable winter and the return of his beloved cow have gone up in the flames.

Now Patsy will have to be sold. Back to the Frumps the farmer goes.
With heavy heart, he makes the trade.

Another cold winter settles in. How the farmer misses his animal friends!

After winter comes the sweetness of spring. The farmer plants…and hopes…and trusts.

He is patient. He perseveres. And when soft rains fall, he kneels in thanks.

His joy returns as the seedlings sprout. He loves to see new life spring forth.

A stretch and a yawn feel good after a long day of work.

Deep beneath his covers, the farmer is soon
lost in a pleasant dream.

Suddenly there is thunder! The farmer wakes with a gasp, "Please, Lord, not again!"

Lightning streaks across the sky and strikes the neighboring fields.

Ablaze! Their land in flames, the Frumps are helpless. Who can help them? Who?

Good efforts are all in vain.

The fields are ruined.

As morning dawns, the Frumps stand humbly before the farmer and thank him for his help. The farmer knows the sadness of his neighbors. What more for them can he possibly do?

Suddenly his eyes open wide in amazement

In the company of his animal friends, the farmer takes comfort, but…

He cannot believe what he sees. He has been visited by a miracle!

Just yesterday, his little garden was not yet ready for harvest. Now it is mature and magnificent!

Tears of joy,

tears of gratitude wash the farmer's face.

He dances and dances, his joy full.

A peaceful smile rests on his face. He now knows what he can do for his neighbors.

Gathering from his overflowing bounty, the farmer creates a most excellent feast, to which he calls his neighbors.

Giving thanks, the farmer invites the Frumps to enjoy themselves at this table.

As they leave, the farmer makes sure they have baskets filled with vegetables and fruits to take home. He is truly a good neighbor and friend.

And for the farmer, the Frumps have a surprise of their own.